W9-AOU-181

# DISNEY FAIRIES

PAPERCUT Z

# Graphic Novels Available from
# PAPERCUTZ

**Graphic Novel #1**

"Prilla's Talent"

**Graphic Novel #2**

"Tinker Bell and the
Wings of Rani"

**Graphic Novel #3**

"Tinker Bell and the Day
of the Dragon"

**Graphic Novel #4**

"Tinker Bell to the Rescue"

**Graphic Novel #5**

"Tinker Bell and
the Pirate Adventure"

**Graphic Novel #6**

"A Present for Tinker Bell"

**Graphic Novel #7**

"Tinker Bell the
Perfect Fairy"

**Graphic Novel #8**

"Tinker Bell and her Stories
for a Rainy Day"

**Tinker Bell and
the Great Fairy Rescue**

**Graphic Novel #9**

"Tinker Bell and her
Magical Arrival"

**Graphic Novel #10**

"Tinker Bell and the
Lucky Rainbow"

*Coming Soon:*

**Graphic Novel #11**

"Tinker Bell and the
Most Precious Gift"

---

DISNEY FAIRIES graphic novels are available in paperback for $7.99 each;
in hardcover for $12.99 each except #5, $6.99PB, $10.99HC.
#6-11 are $7.99PB $11.99HC. Tinker Bell and the Great Fairy rescue is $9.99 in hardcover only
Available at booksellers everywhere.

## See more at www.papercutz.com

Or you can order from us: please add $4.00 for postage and handling for first book, and add $1.00 for each
additional book. Please make check payable to NBM Publishing. Send to: Papercutz, 160 Broadway, Suite 700, East Wing, New York,
NY 10038 or call 800 886 1223 (9-6 EST M-F) MC-Visa-Amex accepted.

# #10 "Tinker Bell and the Lucky Rainbow"

# Contents

**PAPERCUTZ**™
NEW YORK

**"The Enchanted Gem"**
Script: Carlo Panaro
Revised Dialogue: Cortney Faye Powell
and Jim Salicrup
Pencils: Antonello Dalena
Inks: Manuela Razzi
Color: Kawaii Creative Studio
Letters: Janice Chiang
Page 5 art:
Concept: Tea Orsi
Pencils and Inks: Sara Storino
Color: Andrea Cagol

**"Tinker Bell and the Lucky Rainbow"**
Concept and Script: Paola Mulazzi
Revised Dialogue: Cortney Faye Powell
and Jim Salicrup
Layout: Anna Merli
Pencils: Sara Storino
Inks: Marina Baggio
Color: Litomilano
Letters: Janice Chiang
Page 31 Art:
Concept: Tea Orsi
Pencils and Inks: Sara Storino
Color: Andrea Cagol

**"A Winter Fairy Concert"**
Concept and Script: Augusto Macchetto
Revised Dialogue: Cortney Faye Powell
and Jim Salicrup
Layout: Anna Merli
Pencils: Sara Storino
Inks: Marina Baggio
Color: Litomilano
Letters: Janice Chiang
Page 18 Art:
Concept: Tea Orsi
Pencils and Inks: Sara Storino
Color: Andrea Cagol

**"The Vain Flower"**
Script: Tea Orsi
Revised Dialogue: Cortney Faye Powell
and Jim Salicrup
Layout: Antonello Dalena
Pencils: Manuela Razzi
Inks: Marina Baggio
Color: Studio Kawaii
Letters: Janice Chiang
Page 44 Art:
Concept: Tea Orsi
Pencils and Inks: Sara Storino
Color: Andrea Cagol

Nelson Design Group, LLC – Production
Special Thanks – Shiho Tilley
Michael Petranek – Associate Editor
Jim Salicrup
Editor-in-Chief

ISBN: 978-1-59707-367-7 paperback edition

ISBN: 978-1-59707-368-4 hardcover edition

Copyright © 2012 Disney Enterprises, Inc. All rights reserved.

Printed in Singapore.
December 2012
by Tien Wah Press PTE LTD
4 Pandan Crescent
Singapore 128475

Distributed by Macmillan

First Papercutz Printing

# THE ENCHANTED GEM

IF YOU HEAD TOWARD THE SECOND STAR ON YOUR RIGHT AND FLY STRAIGHT ON TILL MORNING, YOU'LL COME TO *NEVER LAND*, A MAGICAL ISLAND WHERE MERMAIDS PLAY AND CHILDREN NEVER GROW UP.

WHEN YOU ARRIVE, YOU MIGHT HEAR SOMETHING LIKE THE TINKLING OF LITTLE BELLS. FOLLOW THAT SOUND AND YOU'LL FIND *PIXIE HOLLOW,* THE SECRET HEART OF NEVER LAND AND HOME OF TINKER BELL AND ALL HER FAIRY FRIENDS.

SOMETIMES *LOST OBJECTS* FROM THE MAINLAND ARE WASHED IN WITH THE TIDE ONTO THE BEACHES OF NEVER LAND...

...AND TINKER BELL IS THERE TO GREET THEM...

I JUST *LOVE* FINDING LOST THINGS!

CAN'T WAIT TO SEE WHAT *WONDERS* I'LL COME ACROSS TODAY!

- 9 -

- 12 -

- 14 -

- 15 -

# THE WINTER FAIRY CONCERT

THE **WINTER FAIRIES** HAVE JUST RETURNED TO **PIXIE HOLLOW,** BUT THEY'LL BE LEAVING AGAIN SOON...

...SO ALL THE OTHER FAIRIES ARE WORKING HARD ON PREPARING A SPECIAL CELEBRATION JUST FOR THEM!

IT'S GOING TO BE AN AMAZING CONCERT!

WOW, LOOK AT THOSE WONDERFUL MUSICAL INSTRUMENTS!

CROAK!

CAREFUL, FAWN, THESE INSTRUMENTS ARE *FRAGILE.*

DON'T WORRY, TINK! I'M BEING VERY CAREFUL!

PLING

- 22 -

- 24 -

- 27 -

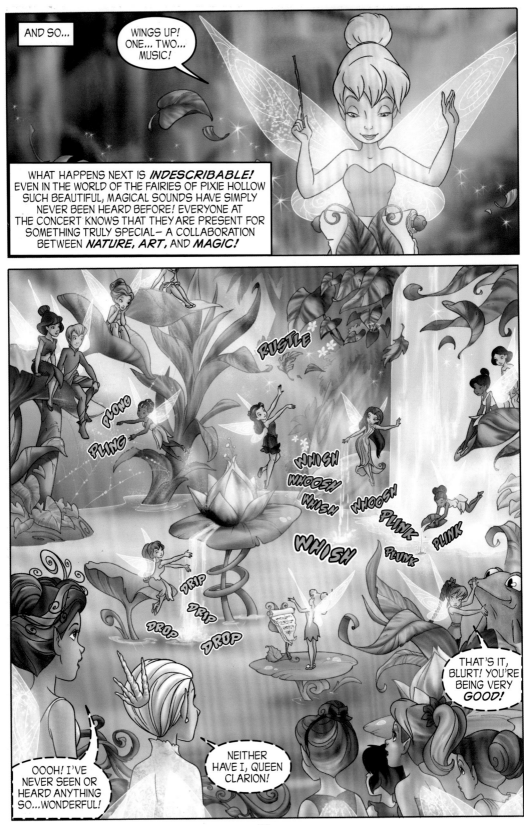

AND SO...

WINGS UP! ONE... TWO... MUSIC!

WHAT HAPPENS NEXT IS *INDESCRIBABLE!* EVEN IN THE WORLD OF THE FAIRIES OF PIXIE HOLLOW SUCH BEAUTIFUL, MAGICAL SOUNDS HAVE SIMPLY NEVER BEEN HEARD BEFORE! EVERYONE AT THE CONCERT KNOWS THAT THEY ARE PRESENT FOR SOMETHING TRULY SPECIAL— A COLLABORATION BETWEEN *NATURE, ART,* AND *MAGIC!*

RUSTLE

PLONG
PLUNG

WHISH
WHOOSH
WHISH
WHOOSH
WHISH
PLUNK
PLUNK
PLUNK

DRIP
DRIP
DROP
DROP

THAT'S IT, BLURT! YOU'RE BEING VERY *GOOD!*

OOOH! I'VE NEVER SEEN OR HEARD ANYTHING SO...WONDERFUL!

NEITHER HAVE I, QUEEN CLARION!

# TINKER BELL AND THE LUCKY RAINBOW

THERE'S ALWAYS SOMETHING WONDERFUL TO DO IN PIXIE HOLLOW! TODAY, FOR EXAMPLE, IT'S TIME TO PAINT THE SPOTS ON LADYBUGS' WINGS! THE LADYBUGS WAIT PATIENTLY IN LINE TO GET THEIR LUCKY SPOTS, WHICH TAKE A SPECIAL TALENT TO PAINT...

A TINKER-TALENT FAIRY AT YOUR SERVICE, FAWN!

THAT'S GREAT, TINK! I CAN ALWAYS USE THE HELP!

JUST ANOTHER SPOT OF BLACK AND WE'RE ALL DONE WITH YOU, PRETTY GIRL!

BZZ!

YOU HAVE SO MANY LADYBUGS TO PAINT, I FIGURED YOU COULD USE A HANDY DEVICE LIKE THIS!

YOU'RE UP, LADY! AWW, DON'T GIVE ME THAT LOOK!

*GULP!*

- 34 -

- 35 -

- 38 -

- 39 -

- 40 -

- 41 -

# THE VAIN FLOWER

ONE OF THE THINGS, AMONG MANY, THAT FAIRIES ARE KNOWN FOR IS THEIR CELEBRATIONS! TINK, ALONG WITH FAIRIES OF ALL TALENTS ARE NOW PREPARING FOR TOMORROW'S BIG PARTY IN *SPRINGTIME SQUARE!*

THERE'S NOTHING I ENJOY MORE THAN *TINKERING!* I CAN'T WAIT TO TURN THESE *LOST OBJECTS* INTO SOMETHING *FABULOUS!*

TOCK TOCK

BUT SUDDENLY...

TINK!

ROSETTA! WHAT'S WRONG?

IT'S A *FLOWER EMERGENCY!* YOU NEED TO COME WITH ME TO--

-- *SPRINGTIME SQUARE!* I DIDN'T KNOW WHO ELSE TO TURN TO--!

YOU KNOW YOU CAN *ALWAYS* COUNT ON ME!

FOR TINKER BELL, *FRIENDS* ALWAYS COME *FIRST!*

# WATCH OUT FOR PAPERCUTZ™

Welcome to the tenth (technically the eleventh, if you count TINKER BELL AND THE GREAT FAIRY RESCUE), tender-hearted DISNEY FAIRIES graphic novel from Papercutz, those pixies dedicated to magically creating great graphic novels for all ages! I'm Jim Salicrup, the Editor-in-Chief and part-time pretend pirate. ARRR.

When I was just a child, one of my dreams was to work in comics. I didn't know then that I'd wind up being an editor, as most people have no idea exactly what a comicbook editor does, and I didn't have a clue back then either. I probably hoped to become a comicbook artist, as I loved drawing, and I just loved the artwork found in all my favorite comics. It was great fun to study the artwork and discover the subtle differences in various artists' styles, as no two artists tend to draw exactly alike.

We've been super-fortunate to have many amazing artists in the pages of DISNEY FAIRIES, each one offering their own magical take on Tinker Bell and her friends. The first artist of this illustrious group whose work I've been able to identify is Antonello Dalena. You can see two great examples of his layout artistry in "The Enchanted Gem" and "The Vain Flower" in this volume of DISNEY FAIRIES. The reason I'm able to spot his work is that we're also publishing two other graphic novel series illustrated by the prolific Mr. Dalena at Papercutz: SYBIL and ERNEST & REBECCA. So, to help you become more familiar with Antonello's work, here's a little checklist of previous stories he's drawn in DISNEY FAIRIES:

In DISNEY FAIRIES #7 "Tinker Bell the Perfect Fairy" Antonello, working with Manuela Razzi, penciled "No Need for Words" and "Tink, the Perfect Fairy." In DISNEY FAIRIES #9 "Tinker Bell and her Magical Arrival" Antonello penciled all four stories based on the hit DVD, "The Magical Arrival," "A New Talent,""The Magic in You," and "A Fairy May be Near."

On the following pages we thought you might enjoy seeing a few pages from ERNEST & REBECCA #3 "Grandpa Bug," about a six-and-a-half year old girl, and her best friend, who is a microbe named Ernest. Following that, we've got a special preview of DISNEY FAIRIES #11 "Tinker Bell and the Most Precious Gift."

So, while I didn't grow up to be a fantastic artist like Antonello Dalena, I did get to become an editor who gets to enjoy his work, and all the other great artists published by Papercutz. So, if you want your dreams to come true too, remember to keep believing in "faith, trust, and pixie dust"!

Jim

## STAY IN TOUCH!

EMAIL:        salicrup@papercutz.com
WEB:          www.papercutz.com
TWITTER:      @papercutzgn
FACEBOOK:     PAPERCUTZGRAPHICNOVELS
REGULAR MAIL: Papercutz, 160 Broadway, Suite 700, East Wing, New York, NY 10038

Guillaume Bianci – Writer Antonello Dalena – Artist Cecilia Giumento -- Colorist © DALENA – BIANCO – ÉDITIONS DU LOMBARD (DARGAUD-LOMBARD S.A.) 2011

Don't miss ERNEST & REBECA #3 "Grandpa Bug," available at booksellers now.

Don't miss DISNEY FAIRIES #11 "Tinker Bell and the Most Precious Gift"!

# More Great Graphic Novels from PAPERCUTZ™

## NANCY DREW AND THE CLUE CREW #1

"Small Volcanoes"

The adventures of 8 year-old Nancy Drew!

## ERNEST & REBECCA #4

"The Land of Walking Stones"

A 6 ½ year old girl and her microbial buddy against the world!

## GARFIELD & Co #7

"Home for the Holidays"

As seen on the Cartoon Network!

## MONSTER #4

"Monster Turkey"

The almost normal adventures of an almost ordinary family... with a pet monster!

## THE SMURFS #13

"Smurf Soup"

There's big trouble brewing in the Smurfs Village!

## ARIOL #1

"Just a Donkey Like You and Me"

Meet Ariol, a donkey with blue glasses, trying to survive life at school.

Available at better booksellers everywhere!

Or order directly from us! NANCY DREW AND THE CLUE CREW is available in paperback for $6.99, in hardcover for $10.99; ERNEST & REBECCA is $11.99 in hardcover only; GARFIELD & Co is available in hardcover only for $7.99; MONSTER is available in hardcover only for $9.99; THE SMURFS are available in paperback for $5.99, in hardcover for $10.99; ARIOL is available in paperback only for $12.99.

Please add $4.00 for postage and handling for the first book, add $1.00 for each additional book.

Please make check payable to NBM Publishing. Send to: PAPERCUTZ, 160 Broadway, Suite 700, East Wing, New York, NY 10038 Or call 800-886-1223, 9AM-6PM EST, M-F